Favourite Stories

PaRragon

Bath · New York · Singapore · Hong Kong · Cologne · Delhi · Melbourne

First published by Parragon in 2009
Parragon
Queen Street House
4 Queen Street
Bath BA1 1HE, UK

ISBN 978-1-4075-7591-9

Printed in China

It's time to join your
friends from the Hundred-Acre
Wood in this wonderful tale of
Winnie the Pooh and Tigger too!
Find out just how much Tiggers
like to bounce!
Now turn the page and
begin the adventure!

W innie the Pooh lived in an enchanted place called the Hundred Acre Wood. One day, while he was thinking in his thoughtful spot, he was bounced by a springy character with stripes.

"Hello, Pooh. I'm Tigger! T-I-double Guh-ER!"

"I know. You've bounced me before."

Tigger liked to bounce, especially on unsuspecting friends. Piglet was sweeping leaves when Tigger bounced him. All the leaves went flying. "Hello, Piglet! That was only a little bounce, you know. I'm saving my best one for Rabbit." And Tigger bounded over to Rabbit's house.

Rabbit was happily working in his
vegetable garden when Tigger called out
a greeting. "Hello, Long Ears!"
"No, no, Tigger! Don't bounce …!"
But Rabbit couldn't stop Tigger from
bouncing. Vegetables went flying in all
directions.

A very discouraged Rabbit sat down on the ground. "Tigger, just look at my beautiful garden."

"Yuck! Messy, isn't it?" Tigger frowned in disgust.

"Messy? It's ruined! Oh, why don't you ever stop bouncing?"

"Why? That's what Tiggers do best!" And off Tigger bounced down the road.

Rabbit was so upset about his garden that he called a meeting at his house, which Pooh and Piglet attended.

"Attention, everybody! Something has got to be done about Tigger's bouncing. And I have a splendid idea."

"We'll take Tigger for a long explore in the woods and lose him. And when we find him, he'll be a more grateful Tigger, an 'Oh, how can I ever thank you for saving me' Tigger. And it will take the bounces out of him."

It was agreed. The next morning, Pooh, Piglet and Rabbit took Tigger for an early misty-morning walk in the woods. Tigger bounced up ahead.

Then, when Tigger wasn't looking, Rabbit, Pooh and Piglet hid in a hollow log.

It wasn't long before Tigger noticed he was
lone. "Now where do you suppose old Long Ears
went to? Hallooo! Where are you fellas? Gee, they
must have gotten lost." And Tigger bounced off to
nd his friends.

When all seemed clear, Rabbit crept out of the log and called the others to join him. "You see? My splendid plan is working! Now we'll go and save Tigger."

But as they walked on, they kept coming back to the same sand pit. Pooh, who is a bear of very little brain, had a thought. "Maybe the sand pit i. following us, Rabbit."

"Nonsense, Pooh. I know my way through the
forest." And Rabbit left to prove he could find his
way home.

After Rabbit had been gone awhile, Pooh felt a
rumbling in his tummy. "I think my honey pots
are calling to me. Come on, Piglet. My tummy
knows the way home."

Just then, who should appear but Tigger.
He happily bounced Pooh and Piglet. "I thought
you fellas were lost!"

It turned out that the only one who was lost
was Rabbit! All alone in the dense woods, he
jumped at every noise.

Rabbit grew more and more frightened. The thick mist was filled with strange shapes and sounds.

Suddenly he heard "Halloo!" Before he knew it, Rabbit was found, and bounced, by an old familiar friend.

"Tigger! But you're supposed to be lost!"

"Oh, Tiggers never get lost, Bunny Boy. Come on, let's go home." Rabbit took hold of Tigger's tail, and Tigger bounced him all the way home. This time, Rabbit didn't seem to mind a bit.

Chapter 2

Before long, winter came and transformed the Hundred Acre Wood into a playground of white fluffy snow. Roo was so anxious to play with Tigger that his mother, Kanga, barely had time to tie a scarf around his neck. "Have him home by nap time, Tigger."

"Don't worry, Mrs. Kanga. I'll take care of the little nipper." Then off they bounced, because that's what Tiggers and Roos do best!

Soon they came upon a frozen pond where Rabbit was skating gracefully on the ice. Roo watched in amazement.

"Can Tiggers skate as fancy as Mr. Rabbit?"

"Sure, Roo. Why, that's what Tiggers do best!"

But when Tigger ran onto the ice, he slipped and skidded right into Rabbit, and they all went crashing right through Rabbit's front door!

Tigger groaned. "Tiggers don't like ice skating."

Tigger and Roo looked for something else that Tiggers do best. Roo had an idea. "I'll bet you could climb trees, Tigger!"

"Tiggers don't climb trees. They bounce 'em!"

So Tigger and Roo bounced all the way to the top of a tall tree. Suddenly Tigger realized just how far down the ground actually was. "Whoaa! Tiggers don't like to bounce trees!"

Roo, however, thought this was great fun. He swung back and forth, holding onto Tigger's tail. "Wheee-ee!"

"Stop, kid! S-T-O-P! You're rocking the forest!"

While Tigger was up in the tree, Pooh and Piglet were down below, tracking footprints in the snow. Piglet asked Pooh what they were tracking. "I won't know until I catch up with it."

Just then, Pooh and Piglet heard a sound in the distance. "Halloo!" Pooh turned to his friend. "I hope it isn't a fierce jagular. Because they 'Halloo' and then drop on you."

But it wasn't a jagular at all. It was only Tigger and Roo up in the tree.

Pooh looked up. "How did you and Tigger get way up there?"

"We bounced up!"

"Well, then, why don't you bounce down?" Pooh was very smart for a bear of very little brain. And so, Roo bounced down.

But Tigger was still too frightened to jump that far. "Somebody, help!"

It wasn't long before word got to Christopher Robin that Tigger was in trouble.

Everyone quickly came to his rescue, but no one knew what to do. So I stepped in to help. "You see, Tigger? All your bouncing has finally gotten you in trouble."

"Who are you?"

"I'm the narrator."

"Oh. Well, narrate me down from here. If you do, I promise I'll never bounce again!"

So I turned the book sideways, and Tigger slid right down the block of type to land safely on the ground.

Tigger was most relieved to be on solid ground again.

"I'm so happy, I feel like bouncing!"

Rabbit crossed his arms.

"No, Tigger. You promised!"

"You mean, not even one teensy-weensy bounce?"

When Rabbit shook his head, Tigger turned and walked away.

Roo tugged at Kanga's arm. "Mama, I like the old bouncy Tigger best."

And everyone agreed. So they gave Tigger his bounce back and he leaped for joy. Even Rabbit had to admit it. "Yes, I quite agree. A Tigger without his bounce is no Tigger at all."